Mischa Damjan

ATUK

Pictures by Gian Casty

PANTHEON BOOKS

For Elisabeth Mierta Ursina

First Pantheon Books Edition, 1966
Second Pantheon Books Edition, 1967

© 1964 by Micha Damjan und Nord-Süd Verlag
© 1964 by Mischa Damjan

Library of Congres Catalog Card Number: 66-12455

Printed by s.p.a. Officine grafiche Poligrafici il Resto del Carlino
Bologna (Italy)

It was far, far up in the north.

When the big salmon migrated up the river, Pakkak said to his son: "Atuk, today you are five years old." He gave Atuk a little brown dog and a gay painted sled. Atuk was delighted. He named his little husky Taruk and loved him from the first moment.

Atuk and Taruk played happily together. Often Atuk tied the little dog to his sled and Taruk pulled him along playfully. Since Taruk had not yet learned how to pull a sled, he ran first to the right, then to the left, and the sled swerved to and fro. Mostly Atuk tumbled into the deep snow and Taruk ran away with the empty sled.

Sometimes they raced over the white snowfields. They loved to run after the snowflakes which the wind blew along in front of

them. But most of all, Atuk loved to throw a piece of wood far away. Then Taruk shot like an arrow to fetch it and bring it back to his friend.

They played wild and wonderful games. The little brown dog went everywhere with Atuk, so Atuk was never alone in the wide snow. Taruk was a good friend and a joyful playmate.

When they got tired, they crawled into the igloo and rested close to each other.

Many happy days went by. Then came the time of the seal hunt. Atuk begged his father to hitch Taruk to the big sled with the other dogs. He thought Taruk should get used to long journeys and should learn to pull the sled with the team. For later, Taruk must become a good team husky, strong and tough. Some day Atuk would have his own big sled and his own huskies, and Taruk would become the lead dog. That was Atuk's dream.

So Pakkak did take Taruk with him on the seal hunt. Days and weeks went by. Atuk stood for hours in front of his igloo and looked over the endless snowfields. He longed for his little friend.

One day at last, Atuk heard from far away the gay barking of the dogs. They were coming home at racing speed. Atuk's heart was throbbing wildly. Soon he would be able to pet his Taruk.

Finally they were there! But Atuk was terrified. He couldn't see Taruk anywhere.

"Atuk, the wolf has bitten your dog to death," said his father.

Atuk was silent. His eyes searched sadly over the snow desert, as though he did not believe Pakkak's words. "You can have my best dog," his father said, trying to console him. Atuk silently shook his head.

"Take the black one with the white spots, or the golden brown." Atuk said nothing.

"Or the silvery gray!" The silvery gray husky was beautiful. It was Pakkak's favorite dog. Atuk knew that. But still he said nothing. He only shook his head and looked sadly over the snow-fields.

"I want to kill the wolf!" Atuk said suddenly.

Now Pakkak said: "Atuk, you are not even as tall as the dwarf birch on the hillside. You cannot kill the wolf!"

Atuk went away sadly. He did not want another dog, not even his father's favorite dog. He wanted Taruk. But Taruk had been killed by the wolf. "I want to kill the wolf. I must kill him!" he kept saying.

Was he really as small as his father said?

When the snow had melted, Atuk went to the dwarf birch on the hillside and stood beside it. Disappointed, he went to Pakkak and said: "You were right, father. I am not as tall as the dwarf birch on the hillside."

"Try hard with your bow and arrow. Learn to drive a husky-team and guide your kayak well. You will grow tall and strong." Atuk looked up at his father. "And when you are tall and strong, then you can kill the wolf."

That summer Atuk stalked the tundra with his bow and arrow. He learned how to creep up on the wild birds noiselessly. Soon he was able to tell the difference between the calls of wild geese and wild ducks. He could recognize coots and loons from far away.

In his kayak, Atuk could shoot the wildest rapids. He swam for hours in the river and every day he felt stronger.

Winter came. Atuk cracked his whip and crossed the snow-fields on his sled. He had learned a lot. He could read the signs of the winds, he knew where the ice was strong enough for him and his dogs to cross over the river.

And he practiced throwing his spear. To kill the wolf!

Summers and winters passed. Atuk still mourned for Taruk.

One day he went again to the dwarf birch on the hillside and stood beside it. Then he went to his father and said proudly: "Father, I am bigger than the dwarf birch on the hillside!" Now Atuk slung his bow over his shoulder, put his arrows into his big sealskin pocket, and went to the tundra.

Atuk killed arctic hares and snow partridges. He got wild ducks and geese, coots and loons. Atuk hunted whatever he wanted to hunt. One day he even got a stag with big antlers.

"Atuk is strong," everybody said. "Atuk is the best of the young hunters." Atuk was admired. Atuk was envied.

Soon the snow was back again. It fell and fell and covered the fields, the dwarf birch, and even the sun.

Now Atuk dared to lie in wait for the arctic fox. That was the most difficult task of all. Atuk went into the night with his bow and arrow. Light-footed, he edged near the place where he suspected the fox would be.

And there he saw it. Not far from a snowdrift stood the fox, peaceful and motionless. Atuk came closer and closer. Now he could almost touch it.

"Why are you so calm? Are you not afraid I'll get your precious fur?" Atuk asked, astonished. "Are you not afraid of the hunters?"

Calmly the arctic fox looked at him and said: "No, not any more. For years I fled from the hunters and I always won against them. None of them ever caught me. The animals admired me. They praised me for being quick and clever, fast and cunning. They praised and envied me. But I was always alone."

"And now?" Atuk asked wonderingly.

"Now everything has changed. Now I have a friend!" said the fox and he looked up at a big star in the sky.

"What? A star! But it is so far away. You cannot even play with it!" Atuk cried.

"I don't need to. Every night I wait for it and I know it will come. And when it stands there I look up at it and it looks down to me. So we are together and we are happy."

Atuk didn't say another word. Silently he made his way back to his igloo.

Soon the snow began to melt. More than ever Atuk wanted to kill the wolf. Again he went to the dwarf birch on the hillside and stood beside it. Again he came to Pakkak. "Father, I am twice as big as the dwarf birch on the hillside now," he said, and he took his spear. The wind was howling. The snow owls were swooping in noiseless flight. Atuk braved the storm.

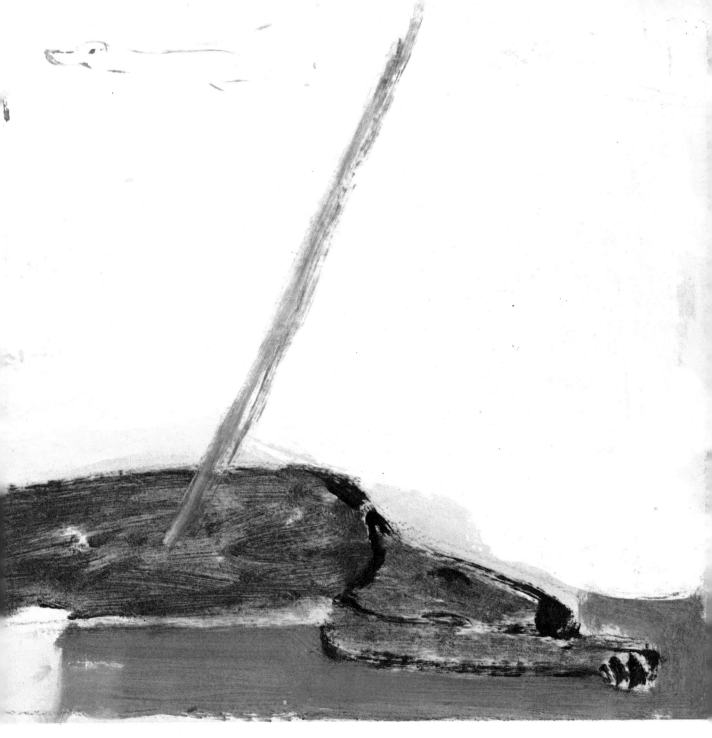

He went to the dark tundra and he killed the wolf.

Now the wolf was lying dead before him. But Atuk was not happy. He was even sadder than before. His little dog Taruk was dead. The wolf was dead. The tundra lay empty and silent before him. Nothing had changed. He had killed the wolf, but Taruk had not come back to him.

Slowly the big round sun defeated the snow and gave the tundra a bright summer dress. Atuk wandered with his spear in his hand and his bow over his shoulder. Now the sun was shining warm and the tundra had a tempting beauty. But Atuk was sad and did not see it. He was thinking of the peaceful arctic fox and his star. The fox had a friend to wait for. But who could Atuk wait for? All the animals of the tundra were hiding from him. To all of them he was the big enemy, the fearsome hunter. Nobody was his friend.

Sadly Atuk walked about the tundra. Suddenly he stood before a flower.

"How delicate it is!" he thought. "And it is not even able to defend itself. I could just stamp it under my foot and crush it."

"Aren't you afraid of me?" Atuk asked crossly.

The flower shook its head.

"I am Atuk, the feared hunter of the tundra!"

The flower was silent.

Don't you envy me?" Atuk asked a little more gently.

The flower shook its head.

"Are you so content?" Atuk asked, astonished.

"Oh no!" the little flower said at last. "I would like to have a friend who would wait for me as long as the big snow lies over the tundra and I lie hidden in my bulb under the ground."

Atuk was silent for a long while. Then he dropped his spear.

"I will wait for you, little flower. Through the whole long winter I will wait for you, until the sun drives away the snow. And when you are back again I will take care of you. I will admire you. I will protect you from the rough wind and I will see that the hunting animals do not tread on you. Yes, I will wait for you," whispered Atuk, as he knelt beside the little flower.